PJ MASKS

Race to the Moon!

Based on the episodes
"Moonstruck, parts 1 and 2"

Ready-to-Read

Simon Spotlight
New York London Toronto Sydney New Delhi

SIMON SPOTLIGHT
An imprint of Simon & Schuster Children's Publishing Division
1230 Avenue of the Americas, New York, New York 10020
This Simon Spotlight edition July 2018
Adapted by Natalie Shaw from the series PJ Masks

For information about special discounts for bulk purchases, please contact Simon & Schuster Special Sales at 1-866-506-1949 or business@simonandschuster.com.
Manufactured in the United States of America 0518 LAK
10 9 8 7 6 5 4 3 2 1
ISBN 978-1-5344-2204-9 (hc)
ISBN 978-1-5344-2203-2 (pbk)
ISBN 978-1-5344-2205-6 (eBook)

This looks like a job

for the PJ Masks!

Greg becomes Gekko!

Connor becomes Catboy!

Amaya becomes Owlette!

They are the PJ Masks!

Now Luna Girl can travel
to the moon.
The harvest moon makes her
Luna Magnet stronger!

She wants to find the
harvest moon crystal.
It will make her so strong
that no one can stop her!

The PJ Masks have to go to the moon to stop Luna Girl.

PJ Robot can help.

He turns Headquarters into a rocket ship!

PJ Masks are on their way into space to save the day!

Then Luna Girl throws
energy bubbles at their ship.

Owlette tries to keep the ship safe.

It does not work!

They have to land on the moon.

Luna Girl is on the moon too!

The PJ Masks race out on their PJ Rovers.

They are too late.
Luna Girl finds the
harvest moon crystal!

The PJ Masks have to stop her!
Catboy tries to use his Super Cat Speed.

It does not work!

Luna Girl laughs.

Their powers
do not work the same
on the moon.

Luna Girl uses the crystal
to make a trap
around the PJ Masks.

They escape
when Gekko uses his
Super Gekko Muscles!

The heroes break free from the trap!

They work together to get
the harvest moon crystal.

The PJ Masks saved
the moon!